Diane Marcial Fuchs

A Bear
for
All Seasons

Illustrated by Kathryn Brown

Henry Holt and Company • New York

Henry Holt and Company, Inc.
Publishers since 1866
115 West 18th Street
New York, New York 10011

Published in Canada by Fitzhenry & Whiteside Ltd.,
195 Allstate Parkway, Markham, Ontario L3R 4T8.

Library of Congress Cataloging-in-Publication Data
Fuchs, Diane Marcial. A bear for all seasons / by Diane Marcial Fuchs;
illustrated by Kathryn Brown.
Summary: Fox comes to visit Bear on a cold winter day,
and they reminisce about the seasons of the year and what
they like best about each one.
[1. Bears—Fiction. 2. Foxes—Fiction. 3. Seasons—Fiction.
4. Friendship—Fiction.] I. Brown, Karhryn, ill. II. Title.
PZ7.F93Be 1994 [E]—dc20   94-44650
ISBN 0-8050-2139-6
First Edition—1995

Printed in the United States of America on acid-free paper.∞

1 3 5 7 9 10 8 6 4 2

The artist used watercolors and color pencil on Windsor & Newton
paper to create the illustrations for this book.

To my parents,
with thanks for providing the woods
—D.M.F.

For my parents, Colleen and Devoe Brown
—K.B.

<big>A</big>lone at last, Bear thought. He rubbed his eyes and yawned. He snuggled beneath his thick quilt.

The winter winds moaned. The trees outside groaned. A log in the fireplace crackled.

Bear smiled and snuggled deeper.

Tap, tap, tap. Bear loved the sound of naked trees tapping against his den.

Scratch, scratch, scratch. He loved the sound of crisp leaves being blown against his door.

Crackle, crackle, crackle. Bear loved to hear the snap and pop of the fire.

Tap, scratch, crackle, crackle.

Scratch, crackle, tap, tap.

Bear's eyelids drooped as he listened to the sounds of winter. Soon he would be fast asleep.

Tap, crackle, scratch.

Bam, bam, BAM!

Bear sat straight up.
BAM, BAM, BAM!
That was *not* a winter sound!

Bear put on his robe and peeked out the window.
"Get out of bed!" a voice called.
Bear padded to the door and opened it.

His friend, Fox, stamped the snow off his feet and scurried
into Bear's warm den. "A fellow could freeze to death out
there," Fox said. "Where *were* you?"

"Sorry, Fox," Bear said. "I was just about to take my long winter nap." Bear's eyelids felt as heavy as iron skillets. He wished Fox would leave—and soon!

Fox rubbed his paws together. "Don't you just *hate* winter?"

"Why, no!" Bear replied. "Winter is my favorite season!"
He yawned and stretched. "And now, if you will excuse me . . ."

"Think of spring," Fox said, waving a forepaw. "A south wind warms the earth. Buds smile into delicate leaves. The woods are alive!"

Bear nodded happily at the memory. "It's when I wake up," he said. "I do love to sniff the fresh, green woods."

"Flowers bloom. Bees buzz," Fox continued.

Bear clapped his paws. "And the bees make honey!" Fox frowned. "But then there are the spring rains."

Bear closed his eyes. "Mmmm. Honey and cinnamon on toast. I can taste it now."

"And the ground turns into a mucky mess," Fox complained.

"I've changed my mind," Bear cried. "Spring is *really* my favorite season!"

"You said winter was your favorite."

"I was wrong."

"Are you sure?" Fox asked.

"Yes, I'm certain!" Bear replied.

"Think of summer," Fox said. "The sun warms the ground. Leaves rustle gently in the breeze. The woods are cool and dark."

Bear sighed. "It's a lazy time," he said.

"Squirrels chatter in the trees. Crickets chirp," Fox said.

Bear smiled. "Blackberries are finally ripe!"

"Mosquitoes buzz." Fox paused. "And bite!"

Bear smacked his lips. "How good a fat, juicy blackberry would taste right now!"

Fox continued, "And sometimes it gets so hot! I just lie and pant."

Bear sighed and looked at the ceiling, remembering his summers. "Summer is truly my favorite season," he said.

"You said spring was your favorite."

"I was wrong."

"Are you sure?" Fox asked.

"Yes, I'm certain!" Bear replied.

"Think about autumn!" Fox said. "The awful heat disappears. Leaves turn yellow, red, and orange. The woods are *so* beautiful!"

Bear dabbed the tears in his eyes. "Oh, Fox, fall *is* gorgeous. You know how beauty always makes me cry."

"Leaves crunch underfoot," Fox said. "An earthy smell fills the air."

Bear remembered walks to the stream. "And there are salmon in the river again!" His mouth watered.

Fox scowled. "But too soon the trees are naked. The woods are dull and gray. And the wind blows from the north." He shivered.

Bear could almost smell fish frying in the pan. "Autumn is really and truly my favorite season."

"You said summer was your favorite."

"I was wrong."

"Are you sure?" Fox asked.

"Yes, I'm certain!" Bear replied.

"Think about winter," Fox said. "The earth goes to bed under a pure white blanket of snow. Icicles hang from each branch and bush. The woods are transformed."

Bear stretched and yawned.

Fox continued, "On sunny days the snow glitters like a million diamonds."

Bear laughed. "I love to catch snowflakes on my tongue!"
"How good a steaming, hot drink tastes on such cold
days!" Fox said.

Bear nodded. "How it warms the tummy and toes."
"How good a crackling fire feels!" Fox said.
"It does make one feel toasty." Bear's stomach rumbled.
"Say, Fox, I have an idea! Would you like some hot cocoa?"

"I would love some, Bear. I thought you would never ask."
Bear poured milk into a pan and set it over the fire to
warm. Then he spooned cocoa into two mugs. The trees
outside groaned. The winter winds moaned.

Tap, scratch, crackle, crackle.

"You know, Fox, I was wrong. I love winter," Bear began.
Fox snorted. "But you said . . ."

"And I love spring and summer and autumn. But do you
know what is really and truly my favorite time?"

"No, Bear, tell me. What is your favorite time?"

Bear poured the steaming milk into the mugs and stirred.
"The company of a good friend is what I love best—no matter
what the season."

Fox smiled and sipped his drink. "Are you sure?"
"Yes," Bear replied. "I'm *absolutely* certain!"